Manfred
The Unmanageable Monster

Manfred
The
Unmanageable
Monster

Budge Wilson

illustrated by Jill Quinn

Pottersfield Press, Lawrencetown Beach, Nova Scotia, Canada

Canadian Cataloguing in Publication Data
Wilson, Budge
Manfred the unmanageable monster
ISBN 1-895900-41-7
I. Quinn, Jill II. Title
PS8595.I5813M35 2001 jC813'.54 C2001-900028-6
PZ7.W69004M35 2001

Pottersfield Press gratefully acknowledges the ongoing support of the Nova Scotia Department of Culture and Tourism, Cultural Affairs Division, as well as The Canada Council for the Arts. We acknowledge the financial support of the Government of Canada through the Book Publishing Industry Development Program for our publishing activities.

Pottersfield Press
83 Leslie Road
East Lawrencetown
Nova Scotia, Canada, B2Z 1P8
Website: www.pottersfieldpress.com

To order, phone 1-800-NIMBUS9 (1-800-646-2879)

Printed in Canada

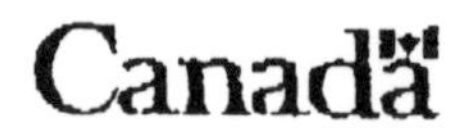

This book is for my friend
Judy Goddard.
— B.W.

For my newest little monster, Jarod.
— J.Q.

EXTRA
STICKY
GLUE
RED
NAIL
POLISH

Chapter 1

Once upon a time, there were two monsters who lived in a bog. This swamp was called the Bog of Monstrosity, and it was the dwelling place for monsters, a few dragons, and other scary things.

The two grown-up monsters in this story were called Marvin and Mildred. Marvin was a very successful monster, who seemed able to be and do all the things that monsters are supposed to be good at. For one thing, he *looked* monstrous. He was very big, and had large round blood-shot eyes, a mouthful of exceptionally sharp teeth, a snorting kind of nose, a furry body, and strong prickly legs.

Mildred was a less perfect monster for several reasons. She had an unfortunate tendency to look friendly from time to time, and to apologize after doing something unusually mean.

Moreover, a few of Mildred's teeth were missing, and her legs were smooth. Prickly legs are a sign of a genuinely talented monster, and Mildred was sensitive about this deficiency. In fact, she occasionally glued rose thorns onto her legs, in order to fool the public. But this only made it more difficult for her when rushing through the underbrush — something that monsters are supposed to do as often as possible.

In order to feel more adequate as a monster, Mildred painted her toes and her claws with bright red nail polish. This drew attention to her really quite marvelously long pointed nails. Few people would have realized that Mildred was not entirely successful as a monster.

In the due course of time, Mildred and Marvin had a child, whom they called Manfred. They named him this because there had once been a Manfred who had been both famous and bad. They hoped that Manfred would grow up to be the most perfect and most admired monster in the Bog of Monstrosity.

Every other parent, of course, had exactly the same ambition. But because Marvin was such a truly impressive monster (and proud of it), and because Mildred was a secret failure (and ashamed of it), both of them (for their own private reasons) wanted Manfred to be unusually monstrous.

Chapter 2

Even as a baby, Manfred was a worry to his parents. For instance, he didn't scream all the time. He made soft gurgly noises and slept a lot. In fact, he slept an *awful* lot. He was furry and bloodshot and prickly in all the right places, but he seemed to have no desire at all to break his crib, to tease dragons, or to stick pins in groundhogs.

In fact, when he was a bit older, there was a groundhog that he even seemed to LIKE. When his parents were away and when there were no neighbors monster-sitting him, he would take the groundhog to bed with him. Furthermore, he hugged the groundhog.

Hugging is something that is absolutely forbidden among monsters. Hitting and kicking are fine; biting is even better. Hugging is regarded as a bad WORD and an even worse DEED.

As Manfred grew older, his parents became more and more concerned about his development. He liked to eat berries, for instance, instead of people. He also moved around slowly instead of roaring and crashing about at top speed. Even with his blood-shot eyes and sharp teeth and prickly legs (and he had an unusually fine growth of prickles), he somehow did not manage to look fierce.

"And a monster who looks friendly," sighed Mildred, thinking sadly of her own problem, "is absolutely useless." Marvin did not sigh. He roared. Snorting through his terrible nose, he howled, "No child of MINE is going to be a failure! This Manfred of yours is going to CHANGE!"

You will notice that he referred to Manfred as Mildred's child. He did not even like to think of Manfred as being his own son. No one as scary, mean, alarming, fierce, and dangerous as Marvin could bear to think of having a sleepy and easy-going son. This sometimes happened to other monsters. Not to Marvin. He would not let it happen.

Chapter 3

Thus it was that Mildred and Marvin undertook to teach Manfred how to become a successful monster. They decided to give him lessons every morning at 3 a.m. sharp. This is a very creepy time of night, and a good hour for lessons in both general and specific monster skills.

They decided to do the teaching in Centerbog — a remote part of The Bog of Monstrosity seldom visited by other monsters. It was wet, unusually dark and filled with scary things.

At exactly three o'clock in the morning (which is really night), Marvin and Mildred came galumphing into Manfred's room, snorting and shrieking and kicking aside the furniture. This did not alarm Manfred, who was actually very brave.

Perhaps brave is not the correct word. Let us put it this way: he wasn't frightened by loud noises or rackety monsters hurrying off to their various terrible deeds; he didn't get upset when his friends kicked him or leapt out from behind bushes, shouting "BOO!"; he didn't jump when he heard loud thunks and roars and screams — or even the gnashing of teeth. These were, after all, the background noises of his life.

Therefore, when Mildred and Marvin came roaring into his room at 3 a.m., he was not alarmed. Nor did he wake up very quickly. He tended to be a little bit sleepy even at noon, so of course he was a whole lot sleepy at 3 a.m.

As soon as Manfred was out of bed, Mildred and Marvin took him out to the middle of Centerbog. They didn't take him by the hand. They pushed and shoved him ahead, howling, in unison, "This is for your own good!"

Manfred didn't mind this. Half of him was asleep, and the other half watched the night birds and listened to the night sounds and thoroughly enjoyed the trip.

When they reached Centerbog, the training began.

Marvin and Mildred showed him how to crash through the bushes — breaking trees and squashing flowers.

They demonstrated eyeball-rolling, throat gurgling, clawing, and stamping. They taught him how to put burrs all through his fur (which they regarded as too soft), and how to sharpen his teeth on the stones beside Centerbog.

Manfred was a quick learner. He did and learned all these things, and he did and learned them well. Marvin and Mildred were delighted. Then they all stormed home, snorting and pushing and thunking along. When they reached home, they went to bed.

Chapter 4

At eight o'clock, Manfred woke up and shuffled into the kitchen for his breakfast of broken clam shells and rose thorns. Mildred and Marvin were sitting there impatiently, eagerly waiting to see the change in their son.

But there was no change. He still looked sleepy; he still moved slowly; he smiled a lot, and insisted on eating the roses as well as the thorns.

Marvin was furious. Mildred pretended to be angry too. But what she

really felt was worried. What future was there for a monster who was not monstrous? She almost bit off one of her long sharp scarlet nails, but stopped just in time.

Marvin stomped up and down on the lumpy floor of their house. "Tonight," he roared, "we will try again!"

And they did. Night after night after night. And each night the lessons got harder and scarier and noisier and longer. Every night Manfred learned his lessons well and did all the things he was supposed to do. Each morning he woke up and was exactly the same as he had always been. Marvin was frantic with rage, and Mildred was so worried that she lost her appetite for raw sea urchins.

It is true that Manfred was sleepy and slow moving and stubborn. But he was not stupid. Furthermore, although patient beyond the limits of all people and most monsters, he knew when he had had *enough*.

He was by now ten years old, and his nightly lessons had gone on for five years. He had lost enough sleep. He was also tired of all that anger and worry that Marvin and Mildred were constantly tossing around. He decided to do something about it.

Manfred went out to his favourite snoozing place on a nice comfortable rock overlooking a sea cliff to the east of The Bog of Monstrosity. There he settled down and had a good refreshing sleep for two hours.

Then he sat up and stared thoughtfully at the sea for half an hour. He had made up his plan. He thought it was a good one. After that he went out to search for his friends.

Manfred had a lot of friends. They pretended, when at home, that they didn't like him. He was definitely a peculiar monster, and it was safer to tell their parents that they disapproved of him. Otherwise the parents might have forbidden them to play with him, lest some of his peculiarity rub off on them.

Usually the monster children met Manfred at Outerbog. Hardly anyone went there because it was so far away — and also because it was a rather pretty place, with buttercups and daisies and some friendly looking trees. It wasn't the sort of place where monsters usually go.

Although the children knew that liking Manfred was dangerous, they all thought he was wonderful. He did such unusual things. He rested. He stared happily into space. He had conversations and thought thoughts instead of forever DOING things. He played with the groundhogs. He ate blueberries. His love of sunsets became infectious. Sometimes as many as fifteen little monsters would meet on the giant fallen tree in Outerbog to watch the sun disappear behind the trees.

If the parents had learned about all this quiet and friendly activity taking place in Outerbog, there would have been BIG TROUBLE. The children would have been locked in their rooms until they had proved that they were sufficiently monstrous to go out again. Marvin and Mildred would have been humiliated beyond belief.

Chapter 5

On this particular morning, Manfred met his friends at Outerbog at the Musing Mound. This was a little hillock of soft moss which had become very popular as a thinking and sorting-out place. Monsters, of course, are never supposed to think, especially on soft pieces of ground.

When they had gathered, Manfred told them of his plan. They listened carefully. When he finished talking, they could see that it was a good idea, not only from Manfred's point of view, but

from their own. Everyone agreed to cooperate, and to keep the plan an ABSOLUTE SECRET. They decided to start on the following morning.

For the rest of that day, the small monsters played in Outerbog — swimming, birdwatching, talking, doing gymnastics over the fallen trees, searching for teaberries.

After leaving Outerbog at suppertime, they became fierce and noisy and gruesome as they approached their houses.

The parents looked out to see their children kicking and pushing and shoving one another as they shrieked and bellowed and roared their way home. They were pleased to see that their children were developing so nicely.

Marvin and Mildred looked out the window and watched the return of Manfred. He ambled slowly along, gently kicking a stone in front of him, stopping to examine the wild roses, whistling softly to himself.

“Curses,” roared Marvin, with his gravelly voice. “Oh dear oh dear oh dear oh dear,” sighed Mildred.

The next day was sunny and warm. Manfred rose from his bed, slowly as usual, and cheerfully ate his breakfast of scrambled rocks and pickled roots. He felt fine and said so. He smiled at his mother and then had a little snooze on the veranda. Then he woke up, yawned, and walked off in the direction of Outerbog. That was at eleven o’clock in the morning. No one would have realized that something special was about to happen.

Chapter 6

At four-thirty, all the small monsters started to return home from their day of playing with Manfred at Outerbog. Millicent, a particularly prickly little monster, came rushing into her house, screaming, "Mother, I'm so scared! I've just been out to Outerbog and I saw Manfred. He scares me so much that I can't STAND it!" Then she kicked the cat and went in to mess up her fur before dinner. She refused to tell her mother why Manfred was so frightening.

At the very moment when Millicent was telling her troubles to her mother, one of the biggest monster children, Murdock, was arriving at his house. His father reached the house at the same time, tired after a hard day at the TV studio where he acted in Monster Movies. Murdock looked depressed, and was sighing heavily.

"What's wrong, son?" asked his father whose name was Morris, kicking him hard to show his affection. Murdock sighed again. Deeply. "Why can't I be as frightening as Manfred?" he groaned. "Why can't I be the terror of Outerbog like he is? Why? Why? Why?" He wouldn't tell his father why Manfred was so scary.

All over the heart of downtown Monstrosity, children were telling their parents of the fearsome qualities of Manfred. They returned home screaming with fear, sighing with envy, stamping with admiration. None of the children would explain why they were so upset.

Parents all over the Bog lay awake that night, worrying about their children. Weren't they brave enough? Why was Manfred so special? Couldn't their own children learn to be as fierce as Manfred?

All these things happened for three days in a row. The monster parents became almost ill with distress and frustration. They stopped thumping and roaring around, and just sat on their bumpy verandas and moaned, with a deep and terrible anxiety.

Finally, one of the parents (Murdock's father, Morris, to be exact) could stand it no longer.

He rose from his chair and shouted out to the neighbors: "Enough of this misery! We must ACT!"

He waved his furry arms and roared his loudest.

"Come! We will have a Bog meeting in Monstrosity Hall. Everyone will come. EVERYONE! This includes Marvin and Mildred and Manfred. We will not leave

MONSTROSITY
HALL

that meeting until we know what it is that makes Manfred such a monstrous monstrosity of a monster!"

Morris pounded down the hill leading to Monstrosity Hall. As he clumped by, people left their houses and followed him. Every single monster came — the parents, the grandparents, the children, even the baby monsters in their mothers' arms.

In the center of the group were Marvin and Mildred — puzzled and nervous and proud. At the end of the line, walking slowly, taking his time, strolled Manfred, chewing thoughtfully on a piece of grass. He looked, as usual, serene and a little bit sleepy.

Chapter 7

The meeting was short and well organized. Morris led the meeting. He gave a short speech outlining the crisis of the past three days. He described the frightened young monsters — their envy, their fear, their admiration, their terror.

"Obviously," Morris concluded, "Manfred has some deep and terrible secret that he should be sharing with all of us. No talent as horrible as his should be locked away in his own head. If we can all be more successful monsters by learning his secrets, then let us do so! Rise, Manfred, and speak!"

Manfred smiled slightly but said nothing.

Secretly, Morris began to feel uneasy.

Finally, Manford's father, Marvin rose. He spoke.

"If you want to know the source of your children's fear," he said, "ask THEM. WE don't know and Manfred refuses to speak. Only the children know."

Morris gravely and fiercely faced the citizens of the Bog of Monstrosity. His eyes roved about the room, glaring at the monster children. He pointed one bony claw at the floor in front of the stage. "Here!" he roared. "Everyone of you! Come HERE!"

They came — one by one and in groups. Some shivered. Others wept quietly. All looked exceedingly frightened. At last they were all assembled.

"Now!" shouted Morris, pounding the desk, "What IS it? What makes Manfred so AWFUL? What is the secret of his terrifying success? TELL US!"

The children turned, as a group, and faced the audience. From left to right, one by one, each child spoke.

The first little monster said, in a loud clear voice:

"We think that Manfred is a terrifying monster because . . . "

The second child said,

"He is sleepy all the time." Her voice trembled as she said the words.

The third child, who was sobbing quietly, managed to get out the words:

"He likes blueberries."

And so on, down the line of shivering young monsters.

"He smiles a lot."

"He doesn't hurry."

"He likes sunsets."

"He has a garden."

"He hugs groundhogs."

"He thinks up fun games."

The list grew. Each child added a new reason for fearing Manfred. Finally the last child spoke:

"The most terrifying thing about Manfred is that he is different from everyone else in the Bog of Monstrosity."

There was a long silence. Marvin kept his chin high, but he felt extremely nervous. Mildred bit off one scarlet claw before she could stop herself.

Chapter 8

The big Hall was very quiet.

Finally Morris spoke. His voice was icy calm. His knotted eyebrows almost covered his stern eyes. He glared at the children.

"If being different from everyone else is what makes Manfred so monstrous," he said, "then get out there — ALL OF YOU — and learn how to be different from everyone else. I would suggest," — and here his voice became louder — "that all of you go far away to Outerbog with Manfred, where there is plenty of room, and where you will not be disturbed."

"MANFRED!" He addressed Manfred sternly, but with an unmistakable tone of respect. "You will go with them to Outerbog and there you will teach them your secrets. Stay all day. Every day. This kind of complicated learning will obviously take a long, long time. Years, maybe. It's up to you. What is your reply, Manfred?" He fixed Manfred with his blood-shot eyes.

"O.K. by me," said Manfred mildly, taking the grass out of his mouth just long enough to reply. "Fine. If that's what you want."

Manfred turned and walked toward the exit at the back of the Hall of Monstrosity. He turned around just before leaving.

"But we won't start today," he said, yawning. "I'm going for a snooze right now, and then I'll have to water my garden. That will keep me busy till suppertime. Tomorrow we will start."

Morris spluttered, and his eyes became particularly red. The Hall was hushed and tense. He began to speak, in a choked-up, stuttery voice. However, all he said was:

"The meeting is adjourned."

Chapter 9

For Marvin and Mildred, this was the happiest moment of their monster lives. They walked up to the exit door and shook hands with the other citizens as they left the building.

The monster children walked home and had a little sleep before supper. Most monsters ate their dinners in complete silence. No one could think of anything to say.

And thus it was that Manfred and the other young monsters went out each day to Outerbog to play their games and

watch their sunsets and pat the groundhogs. The parent monsters felt, on the whole, that the experiment was working well. Certainly their children were acting more and more like Manfred.

Most of the older monsters were too old to change. But a few of them, feeling embarrassed at first, started eating blue-berries and noticing sunsets. After a while, they even stopped feeling silly about it.

Manfred's plan had worked perfectly. However, success didn't go to his head. Just as his earlier failure hadn't troubled him, being famous didn't interest him at all. He was too busy. He had a lot to do. Like taking naps, and watching polly-wogs, and doing handsprings over the tree stumps, and smelling the buttercups. And, of course, thinking.

EXTRA
STICKY
GLUE
MONSTER
RED
NAIL POLISH

Other Pottersfield Books in this series

Budge Wilson
Cassandra's Driftwood
Harold and Harold
The Cat that Barked

Sheree Fitch
Hullabaloo Bugaboo Day
The Other Author Arthur

Lesley Choyce
Famous at Last
Far Enough Island